101 STORIES FOR BOYS

Published in 2012 by

An imprint of Om Books International

Corporate & Editorial Office
A 12, Sector 64, Noida 201 301
Uttar Pradesh, India
Phone: +91 120 477 4100
Email: editorial@ombooks.com
Website: www.ombooksinternational.com

Sales Office
4379/4B, Prakash House, Ansari Road
Darya Ganj, New Delhi 110 002, India
Phone: +91 11 2326 3363, 2326 5303
Fax: +91 11 2327 8091
Email: sales@ombooks.com
Website: www.ombooks.com

ISBN: 978-93-80070-75-9

Printed in India

10 9 8 7 6 5 4 3 2 1

101 STORIES FOR BOYS

An imprint of Om Books International

www.ombooks.com

Contents

1 Happy Hans

Hans was a cheerful boy. He had happily served his master for seven years. Now, Hans left for home. As a farewell gift, his master gave him a lump of gold. During his journey, Hans met a horseman. Seeing the man ride merrily, Hans exchanged his gold for the horse and trotted away. However, when Hans pushed the horse to run faster, he was thrown off.

Then, Hans saw a countryman with a cow. Hans traded his horse for the cow. After some time, Hans stopped at a moor to milk the cow. A butcher passing by told Hans that his cow was too old to be milked. Hans took the butcher's pig in exchange for his cow.

Next, Hans met a mason and exchanged his pig with the mason's grindstones. The heavy stones soon tired Hans. He went to a well to drink water and dropped the stones inside by mistake! Hans ran home, empty-handed but still happy.

2 John Saves the Prince

Once, a king fell very ill. Before dying, he said to his faithful servant, "John! I leave you with a very important task. My son is young. I want you to be his guardian." John nodded his head, his eyes wet with tears. The prince fell in love with a princess. They decided to marry.

One day, John overheard three divine ravens make some predictions. One of them said, "If the prince mounts his horse, a curse will befall him. If someone else kills the horse, the prince will be saved."

The second raven added, "The prince will see a bridegroom dress. If he wears it, his body would melt away. Somebody will have to throw the dress into the fire."

The third raven said, "When the prince dances with the princess, the princess will turn pale. If someone does not kiss her, she will die. If somebody shares these spells with the prince, he will turn into a stone statue."

John decided to sacrifice his life for the prince. He killed the horse and threw the bridegroom's dress in the fire. But when he kissed the princess, the prince sentenced him to death.

John then told him all about the predictions. The prince felt sorry as John turned into a stone statue!

Soon, the prince and his wife were blessed with twin boys. They wished John could come back to life. One day, the statue spoke, "Master! I can come back to life if you sacrifice your twin sons."

The prince was confused and sad. He then decided to pay back John's loyalties. The prince was about to cut his sons' heads when John came back to life. He said, "Master! God has heard your prayers of repentance and sacrifice. I shall always serve you now."

3 St. Peter and Brother Lustig

Brother Lustig was a poor, but kind man. Once he helped a beggar. Now, this was St. Peter in disguise! St. Peter felt sad for Brother Lustig's poverty, so he decided to help him. He would cure people to earn money for Brother Lustig and himself. Now, the king's daughter fell ill. St. Peter placed his hand on her and cured her. He refused the reward for it, but Brother Lustig became greedy and took the money. St. Peter felt sad at this and left Brother Lustig.

Some days later, Lustig tried to cure another princess by himself. He placed his hand on her head but she lay motionless. Magically, St. Peter appeared. He promised to revive her if Lustig stopped being greedy. Brother Lustig agreed at once. St. Peter cured her. Then, he gave Lustig a bag, which had many medicines. With those medicines, Lustig could earn an honest living.

4 God's Angel

Once, a poor man had so many children that he had asked all his relatives to be his children's godparents.

Now he wondered who could be the new baby's godparent!

Soon, he fell asleep and dreamt that he should ask the first person he met to be the godparent. He woke up and went out. He met a stranger and requested him to be the godparent. The stranger agreed and gave him some healing water, which could cure people.

The man took the water and cured the sick and became very rich. The man then went to meet the godparent to thank him. However, when he entered the godparent's house, he saw that the godparent had wings. He had the head of a man and the body of a horse!

Then the man understood that the godparent was actually God's kind angel who had come to earth!

5 Fundevogel and Lina

Once, a carpenter found a boy in the forest. He took the boy home and named him Fundevogel. The carpenter's daughter, Lina, and Fundevogel grew fond of each other. Now, Fundevogel had magical powers. But their cook was envious of Fundevogel.

One day, she told a maid to throw Fundevogel into boiling water. However, Lina heard them and she and Fundevogel escaped together from the house.

The cook sent three servants after them. But, Lina and Fundevogel fooled them twice by changing their form through magic. First, they became a rose tree with Lina the rose and then a church with Lina, the chandelier.

The cook decided to catch them herself. Then, Fundevogel turned into a pond and Lina, the duck. The cook understood their plan. She tried to drink the water but the duck held her head under water and she drowned. Lina and Fundevogel lived happily thereafter.

6 The Merchant and the Dwarf

Once, there was a merchant who had lost his ships at sea. As he stood unhappily near a stream, a dwarf appeared before him.

The dwarf promised him great riches. In exchange, he wanted the merchant's beloved son after twelve years. The merchant agreed thinking the dwarf's promise to be false. However, when he returned home, he found a heap of gold coins in his cupboard. He was rich again.

Twelve years went by. It was time to repay the dwarf. The young son heard of his father's promise. He went fearlessly to meet the dwarf.

The dwarf asked the young boy to sit in a boat. The helpless merchant watched as the boat disappeared down the stream. The boat reappeared on an unknown shore with a beautiful castle. In the castle, the young boy met a beautiful princess. He married her and became the king of the Golden Mountain.

7 The Good Son

Once, there lived a farmer. He had a tiny son, no bigger than his thumb. One day, the farmer went to plough his field. His son wanted to come along. The farmer was afraid to take him. However, the son cried and so he took him along.

On the field, a giant came and took away the tiny son. The helpless farmer tried to put up a fight, but could not stop the giant. The giant looked after the boy for many years, and the boy grew into a young giant. One day, he wanted to return to his father. He set off for his land. The farmer was speechless at seeing the young giant. The giant told the old farmer that he was his son. Then, taking the furrow, he ploughed the large field. And from then on, the young giant was a good son to his old father.

8 Sultan's Friend

There was once a wise dog named Sultan. He was growing old, so his master wanted to shoot him. Sultan made a plan with his friend, the wolf. The wolf pretended to steal the child of Sultan's master. Sultan saved the child and earned his master's trust. Now, the wolf wanted Sultan to allow him to steal some sheep from his master's flock. However, Sultan told his master about the wolf 's plan. The master caught the wolf and beat him up.

The wolf was very angry with Sultan, so, he called Sultan to the forest. He also called the wild boar to teach Sultan a lesson. Sultan went to the forest with a three-legged cat. The wolf and the boar were scared of the strange cat. They ran in fear but the cat bit the boar's ear. The wolf at once made peace with Sultan. Sultan lived happily ever after.

9 The Kind Prince

Long ago, there lived a king with his three sons. One day, a neighbouring king visited him. This king's kingdom had turned to stone under a witch's spell.

The king sent his sons to find the key to break the spell. The sons wandered in the forest but could not find it. Wandering, they reached a lake. There were many beautiful ducks playing and swimming in the lake. The first two sons wanted to kill ducks to eat them.

However, the third son said, "I will not let you kill these innocent ducks." They got annoyed and left him alone. The queen duck heard them and went to the third son. She said, "I am indebted to you. So, I will help you find the key."

She got the key from the bottom of the lake and gave it to him. The third son went back and gave the key to his father. The father was very happy, and so was the neighbouring king!

10 The Giant Slayer

There once lived a brave hunter. One night, he met three giants in the forest. He told them that he had never missed a shot. The giants wanted him to get the princess who lived in a castle outside the forest.

The hunter agreed and went into the castle. Without disturbing anyone, he picked up a sword and returned to the forest. He tricked the giants and chopped off their heads one by one with the sword.

The king heard and proclaimed, "Whoever killed the giants will marry my daughter!" But the princess did not want to marry just anyone and left the palace. She started living in a hut in the forest.

One day, the hunter was passing by. The princess recognised her father's sword. She realised that the brave hunter had killed the giants and agreed to marry him. The two were soon married and lived happily ever after.

11 The Juniper Tree

Once, a lady sat under a Juniper tree. She wished for a child as white as snow and red as an apple. Quite soon, she was blessed with a baby boy. However, the poor lady died soon after.

The boy's stepmother disliked him. Thus, she killed him. Then, she cut him up and made a pie of him and fed it to her husband. The boy's stepsister was very sad to see this. She gathered the uneaten bones and buried them under the Juniper tree.

Soon, a bird, sat on the Juniper tree. She started singing about the boy's death. People gifted her a gold chain, red shoes and a mill-stone, to listen to her song.

She dropped the chain on the father and the shoes on the girl. However, she dropped the millstone on the stepmother's head and killed her.

Suddenly, the boy came alive. He lived happily with his sister and father, thereafter.

12 The Evil are Punished

Once, a wicked old woman's ugly daughter and beautiful stepdaughter met three little men in the forest. The stepdaughter greeted them and shared her food. They gave her three boons. She would become more beautiful, gold coins would fall from her mouth and she would become a queen.

The ugly daughter was rude and did not share her bread. The three little men cursed her thrice; she would turn uglier, slimy toads would fall out from her mouth and that she would die painfully.

Soon, the stepdaughter became the queen and lived happily at the palace. However, the old woman and her ugly daughter managed to trick her and threw her into the pond. The daughter then disguised herself as the queen.

The real queen swam in the pond as a duck. One day, she called out to the king and told him about the trickery. The king sentenced the old woman and her ugly daughter to death, and took his real queen home.

13 The Three Sisters

Once, there lived a young shepherd. As he grew up, the shepherd wanted to get married. He knew three sisters in his neighbourhood. They were all pretty. So he found it difficult to choose one as his wife. Confused, he went to his mother for her opinion.

His mother said, "Invite the three sisters for dinner. Serve them cheese and see how each one of them eats it."

The young shepherd invited the sisters. Later, he watched them eat, carefully. The eldest sister gulped the cheese hurriedly without even peeling off the skin. The younger sister peeled the skin carelessly and wasted a lot of cheese. The youngest sister, however, peeled the skin very neatly without wasting a bit and ate the cheese.

The shepherd described this to his mother. The mother asked her son to marry the sensible and patient youngest sister. The shepherd married the youngest sister, happily.

14 Who Will Marry the Princess?

Once, there was a king whose daughter had been captured by a fierce dragon. So, he announced that whoever rescues the princess, would marry her.

Now, there were four skilful brothers. One was an astronomer, one a tailor, one a thief and the youngest a hunter. They took up the task.

Using his telescope, the astronomer located the dragon on an island. The brothers set out on a ship. When they reached the island, they found the dragon asleep. Quickly, the thief stole the princess and took her away to the ship. Suddenly, they heard the dragon roaring above them and the hunter shot him. He fell down dead on the ship! Alas! The ship broke. The tailor swiftly sewed back the entire ship.

Safe, they returned to the palace. Now, they started arguing about who would marry the princess. In the end, the king decided to reward them with half his kingdom, and find someone else for his daughter!

15 The Complaining Cobbler

Master Pfriem was a cobbler. He was a short and fat man with grey hair. He meddled in everyone else's business, even though he kept busy in his shoe shop. He loved to find fault with everything. He thought that he was always right.

One morning, Master Pfriem woke up and saw that his wife had lit the fire. He rushed to put it out, saying, "The whole house will burn down!" Then, he gobbled his breakfast and ran to his shop.

While Master Pfriem worked on a shoe, his restless eyes looked towards the road. His assistant showed him a shoe. "Bad work," said Master Pfriem.

"Sir, you made it," the assistant said and received a blow behind his ears. None of the assistants worked for more than a month with him!

Then, Master Pfriem saw a crooked beam inserted in the new house being built across the road. He rushed to advise the carpenters. In between, he shouted at a cart-man for overloading his horses. Then, he ran across the road, waving his arms and knocked over a flower-seller's basket. He kept running to correct some other mistake he had spotted.

That night, Master Pfriem dreamed that he was in Heaven. St. Peter allowed him in, saying, "You have a bad habit of finding fault. Don't do it here or you will have to leave." Master Pfriem agreed and wandered around, admiring Heaven and the angels.

Heaven was a busy place. Master Pfriem noticed many things that annoyed him, but he kept quiet. He lost control when he saw two horses harnessed behind a carriage. He shouted, "Stop! This is all wrong!" The next moment Master Pfriem found himself standing outside Heaven's gates. Right then, he woke up, muttering, "Stupid way to harness horses! But Thank God, I am alive!"

16 The Frog Princess

Once, a king had a son, who was a simpleton. The king was worried about the prince's future and sent him away to learn the ways of life. The prince reached the forest and sat near a pond. A frog saw the sad prince and asked him, "What troubles you?"

The prince told the frog his story. The frog took him to the bottom of the pond and introduced him to the other frogs. They all made him a wise human.

Soon, the prince decided to leave for home. The frogs gifted him a female frog. The female frog said, "We have helped you a lot. I want you to kiss me in return."

The kind prince kissed her. Immediately, she turned into a beautiful princess. The prince was very happy and took her to his palace. The king welcomed them both and soon married the prince to the princess.

17 The Golden Box

One night, a small boy dreamt that he had found a golden box. He woke up feeling very happy. It was winter. That day, he went outside to find the golden box. He pulled his cap over his ears and walked on.

Near his house, was a magical forest, full of beautiful trees and whispering sounds! He wished he would meet an elf or the king of trees. Suddenly, his foot struck something hard. He dug in the ground and found a tiny golden box! Then, he saw that something else shone in the mud! Ah, a tiny key! He pushed the key into the hole and opened the box.

Inside, there was light that turned into a beautiful lady. She said, "Little boy, you have released me from a curse. I bless you with happiness always." Then she disappeared.

Her words were true, for the small boy lived happily ever after.

18 The Skilled Brothers

Once, a man told his three sons, "Go and learn a craft. I shall leave my house to the one who is best at his craft." Thus, the boys left home to complete this mission.

The eldest son became a blacksmith, the second son a barber and the youngest son a swordsman. They returned home to show their father their skills.

The eldest son changed the shoes of a galloping horse and impressed his father. The second son saw a running hare and shaved off its whiskers, perfectly.

'Let's see what my youngest does,' the confused man thought. Suddenly it started raining. The youngest son moved his sword so fast that not a drop fell on him and he was completely dry. The man gave his house to the youngest son.

All the sons loved one another as true brothers. Thus, they lived together, happily.

19 The Intelligent Grandson

There was an old man who lived with his son and daughter-in-law and their little son. He was a sweet little boy who loved his grandfather dearly.

The old man would drool while eating, since he had very few teeth left.

One day, seeing his father drool, the son became angry. He made the old man sit behind the stove and gave him a clay bowl to eat in. The old man cried and looked longingly at the good food on the dining table.

After a couple of days, the son saw his own son making a big clay trough. The child saw his father and said, "This is for you and mother. Grandfather only needs a bowl. You and mother will need a trough to eat in."

The son realised that he was treating his father badly. He apologised to his father and said, "Father, from now on, we will all eat together at the dining table."

20 The Stag Prince

Once, a tailor was travelling alone. He had been warned not to travel at night, but he said, "I am lucky. God always takes care of me."

Night descended and he climbed a tree to be safe from wild animals. Suddenly, he heard loud sounds and saw a stag and a bull, fighting. They shook the tree, so he got down for safety. The stag killed the bull and picked up the frightened tailor in his antlers and ran.

When the stag stopped, he put the tailor down gently. Then, the stag pushed open a rock and said, "Hurry! Come inside quickly."

The surprised tailor followed. There was a huge hall behind the rock! There, lying on the ground was a transparent chest with a miniature castle. In another chest was the loveliest maiden he had ever seen.

The tailor lifted the chest lid and in a flash, the maiden awoke, and the stag turned into a handsome man!

"You've broken the curse," said the maiden, who was actually a princess.

The stag was her brother. A wicked magician, who had turned the brother into a stag, had cursed them. The princess was sent into a deep sleep. The castle and kingdom were shrunk and placed inside a chest. Then one day, the wicked magician had turned himself into a bull. The stag saw his chance and chased him and killed him.

"So, this is what happened to us. I have seen you saving me in my dreams," concluded the princess.

The tailor opened the lid of the second chest and a huge castle sprang up. The kingdom grew until everything became as large and wonderful as it should be.

The beautiful princess and the lucky tailor were married. The handsome brother became the king and everyone lived happily.

21 The Village Thief

Once, a man lived in a village with his son. One day, the son stole some sweets. He told his father about the theft; however, his father did not punish him.

Now, the son became confident and stole something or the other every day. After a few years, he was known as the Village Thief and became notorious for big thefts.

One day, the people reported him to the king. The king sent his soldiers to the village to catch the thief. While they were taking the thief to the prison, the father came to meet his son. The son shouted at his father in rage. The father said, "Why are you shouting at me, son?"

He replied, "Parents always stop children from doing wrong things. But, you never stopped me from stealing. You are responsible for me becoming a thief!"

The father realised his fault, but it was too late!

22 The Nine Devils

Once, a man was travelling alone. Soon, St. Peter joined him, disguised as a beggar. The man shared his food with him. When his money finished, the man prepared to beg with St. Peter.

St. Peter revealed his true form and said, "Whatever you wish for, will appear in your knapsack."

That night, the man was troubled by nine devils. He wished they would enter his knapsack.

The next morning, the man took his knapsack, filled with the nine devils, to the ironsmith. The ironsmith beat it till eight devils died. The ninth ran away to Hell.

Many years later, the man died. He accidentally first went to Hell. The ninth devil, who had escaped, opened the door, recognised him and shut the door tight.

The man wished he were in Heaven. Lo, he appeared in Heaven! St. Peter was surprised by his sudden arrival but welcomed him to stay.

23 The Snake Leaves

Once, a youth married a princess. The princess made him promise that he would have to end his life whenever she died.

Unfortunately, very soon, the princess died of an illness. The youth stayed in the room where the princess' body lay. Everybody thought that he would die of hunger.

Suddenly, he saw a snake slither towards the princess' body. The youth hit the snake thrice. Just then, another snake entered the room carrying three leaves. It placed the leaves on the wounds and the dead snake was alive again!

The youth then placed the leaves on the princess' body. She was alive again! He asked his servant to keep the leaves safely.

Sadly, the princess no longer loved the youth and got him killed. However, the youth's servant placed the three snake-leaves on his body. The youth became alive again!

He told the king about the trickery. The king punished the princess.

24 Kribble-Krabble

There was once a magician called Kribble-Krabble. One day, he looked at a drop of puddle-water with a magnifying glass. He saw tiny creatures struggling with each other. Kribble-Krabble added a drop of a witches' blood to see the creatures more clearly. The creatures became pink in colour.

Kribble-Krabble then asked his friend to look through the magnifying glass. The friend looked and saw a terrible sight. The creatures were actually people, and they were beating each other harshly. The ones on top were being pulled down and the ones at the bottom were struggling to come up.

The friend saw the people catch a lame man and quickly eat him up. A girl was sitting quietly hoping for a piece but the people pulled her too and ate her up. The friend said that the drop seemed to be some huge city like Paris or London.

Kribble-Krabble laughed aloud and said, "Ah! It is a drop of puddle-water!"

25 The Careless Merchant

A merchant had travelled to a village fair and sold all his goods. Pleased with his fortune, he heaved bags of silver and gold over his horse and set off. He was in a hurry to reach home by nightfall. He rode as quickly as he could. By afternoon, he felt hungry and the horse needed hay and water.

The merchant stopped at an inn for his night meal. He told the stable boy to feed his horse. The stable boy looked at his horse and said, "Sir, your horse's shoe is loose, because a nail is missing. There is a blacksmith close by. Shall I call him?"

"No," said the merchant, who had quickly eaten his food. "One missing nail, one loose shoe won't matter. I have to go now."

The horse trotted smartly, but gradually slowed down. The merchant whipped him, but the horse started stumbling. Finally, he got off the horse to lessen the weight, but the horse still limped. After a short distance, the horse fell and his loosened shoe fell off. He got up and limped away to eat grass by the wayside.

"Oh God," groaned the merchant. "This is all my fault. I should have called the blacksmith and got the nail fixed. So much delay because of my hurry! I will never reach home tonight! I will have to leave my money unguarded if I go to get some help. Oh, what if someone steals it?"

He thought for a while as to what he could do. Then, he tied his horse to a tree. He covered his bags of gold and silver coins with branches and grass. He started to walk back to the inn to fetch the blacksmith, and pledged never to ignore small but important things in haste.

26 The Sunbeam and the Bird

Once, at the Swedish coast, there was a dark building. Criminals were kept in that building.

One evening, when the sun was setting, a sunbeam entered the cell of one of the prisoners because sun shines upon both, the evil and the good.

The prisoner looked impatiently and angrily at the sunbeam. Then a little bird flew towards the window, for even birds fly to the good and the evil alike.

The bird cried, "Tweet, tweet" and sat near the window. It fluttered its wings, pecked a feather from one wing and then puffed itself out neatly.

The chained prisoner looked gently at the bird. He felt he had some connection with the sunbeam, the bird and the smell of the flowers, which grew under the window of his cell.

Soon, the bird flew away and the sunbeam vanished. Even then, the sunbeam and the bird had touched the heart of the prisoner. He felt sorry for his bad deeds.

27 The Prince and the Wild Man

In an enchanted forest, lived a wild man who had magical powers.

One day, a prince came to the forest for hunting. To test him, the wild man appeared as an old man and begged him for food. The kind prince gave him some food, as well as some gold coins. Satisfied, the wild man reappeared as himself and told the prince that he would always be there to help him.

The prince liked a princess. However, to marry her, he had to catch the magic apple to be thrown by the princess, during the royal tournament. Thus, the prince went to the wild man who gave him a magic outfit and a horse.

The next day, the prince went to the tournament. None of the other suitors could catch the apple! Finally, the prince caught it and married the princess.

The good wild man helped them all his life.

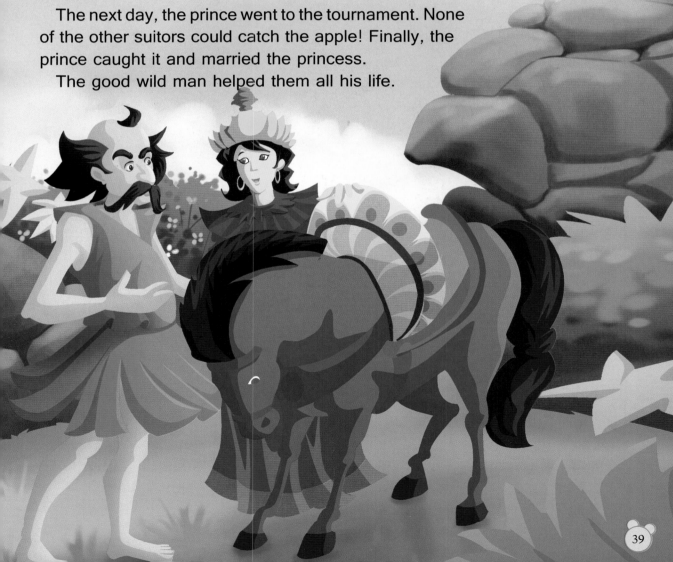

28 The Wicked Prince

There once lived a wicked prince. All he did was conquer countries, frighten people and cause trouble.

Now, the prince had become so full of his victories that he thought, "I am the greatest person and no one is more powerful than me. I can conquer even God." Thus, he ordered his carpenters to construct a powerful ship that would rise above the skies.

Soon, the ship was ready. When it was in the air, God sent an angel to stop it. The wicked prince sent many bullets flying towards the angel. However, nothing happened. The angel shed just one drop of blood, which burnt the entire ship and it went crashing to the ground.

Then, the prince built a better ship. This time God sent gnats. One little gnat got into the prince's clothes and stung him. The wicked prince cried out in pain — he had learned his lesson well!

29 Tuk's Dream

There was once a boy called little Tuk. He had an examination the next day and had to learn the names of all the towns in Zealand.

However, Tuk's parents left him at home to take care of his little sister, so he could not study. When his mother returned, she told Tuk to go help the old washerwoman carry her clothes.

When little Tuk returned and sat down to study, it became dark and there was no light. Thus, he put his geography book under his pillow and slept.

Tuk dreamt of the washerwoman. She said, "You helped me today. I'll help you learn for your test." Then Tuk dreamt of a hen from Kjoge, a parrot from Presto, a knight from Wordingburg and others from all the towns of Zealand.

When Tuk awoke, he couldn't remember his dream. However, as he revised his lesson, he recalled the names of all the towns in Zealand!

30 A Mother's Love

One cold winter, a worried mother sat by her sick child. An old man came to her house to rest. The man was Death.

The mother closed her eyes for a moment to rest but when she woke up, she saw that Death had taken her child away. The mother asked people to help her find Death's house. When she reached, Death had not yet arrived, so she waited.

When Death arrived, the mother begged Death to return her baby. Then Death asked her to look into a well. She saw the future of two children, one whose life was filled with joy and the other's filled with misery. Death told her that one of them was her baby's future.

The mother fell on her knees and prayed to God to take the decision he had made, for it would be for the best. Then, Death carried her baby away. This time the mother did not cry.

31 The Shallow Princess

A prince from a small kingdom wanted to marry the emperor's daughter.

On the prince's father's grave, grew a rose bush with the most beautiful roses. A nightingale sat there, and sang delightfully. The prince sent the roses and the nightingale to the princess but she rejected them.

Then, the prince dressed as a shepherd and made a pot that could tell what every stove was cooking. He gave it to the princess in return for ten kisses. Next, he made a rattle that played every tune there was on earth. However, he was only willing to exchange the rattle in return for a hundred kisses. The princess took that as well.

When the emperor saw the princess with the shepherd, he banished her from the kingdom.

The prince then revealed himself. He was very upset that the princess had rejected precious gifts from a prince, but paid in kisses for simple toys from a shepherd. He also left her and went back to his kingdom.

32 The Giant Turnip

There once lived a rich brother and a poor brother. The poor brother was a turnip farmer. Once, there grew a gigantic turnip in his farm. He gifted the wonderful turnip to the king. The king gave him a lot of wealth.

The rich brother heard about his poor brother's fate. Out of greed, he took many expensive presents for the king. The king gave him the huge turnip in return. He took the turnip helplessly but was jealous of his brother.

Back home, he decided to kill his brother. He trapped him in a sack. Just then, the poor brother screamed, "I have found the sack of wisdom!"

Hearing this, the rich brother himself got into the sack to gain wisdom. However, he found it empty. He realised his mistake and promised that he would never be jealous of anyone. The poor brother forgave him and they lived happily and peacefully.

33 A Boy Learns Ballet

Once, a boy called Peter had a godfather who joined the theatre. Peter often went to watch the dress rehearsals at the theatre. He enjoyed the ballet and sang and enacted the scenes at home. Finally, Peter decided to join a ballet class.

One day, Peter met his mother's dear friend, Miss Frandsen, who was once famous in the theatre. She warned him that the theatre could be a tough place. But Peter was not discouraged. He joined a dancing school. He worked hard under the dance master.

Peter soon got the part of a prince in a show. His proud family came to watch. However, as Peter was dancing, his old dress ripped down the back. All the children laughed and called him Ripperip. Still, Peter did not stop dancing.

Peter was a quick learner and did well in his studies, too. Everyone agreed that this was because Peter knew that it was all right to fail sometimes, and hard work never goes waste.

34 Boarding School

A boy called Jack was to attend a boarding school, far away from home. He went to his boarding school in the train. Herr Gabriel, the owner of the boarding house came to receive Jack.

Along with Herr Gabriel came his five little children and two other boys, Madsen and Primus. The children were falling over each other in their excitement. The other boarders smiled at Jack.

Madame Gabriel welcomed Jack on reaching the house. They ate stuffed turkey for dinner. Jack ate his meal happily and went to his room.

Jack's room looked out into the garden. Through the window, he saw Herr Gabriel come up to the closed window and stick his tongue out. Jack realised that Herr Gabriel was actually looking at his reflection in the windowpanes. Jack had a hearty laugh. He felt the boarding house was not a bad place after all — as the people there were kind and... sometimes funny!

35 The Young Poet

A young man was deeply interested in poetry. He tried to write, but failed every time. He was looking for ideas. Then, he decided to take help from a wise woman. The wise woman lived in a small house with a beehive by the gate. The garden had a potato field, but no trees or flowers.

On seeing her house, the young man felt that it had no poetry. But the wise woman told the young man, it was the thought that mattered. She believed one could catch an idea anywhere.

Hearing her speak, the young man felt inspired. He began to draw ideas from the potatoes in the field. He wanted to write about the history of the potato. Seeing the beehive, he sketched a story on the hardworking bees.

The wise woman's advice helped the young man realise what one can invent, if one catches hold of the idea.

36 The Thistle and the Girl

A garden with beautiful flowers was the pride of a manor house. Outside this garden, near the fence, grew a thistle bush. The thistle bloomed with flowers despite its thorns.

One day, a group of young men and women came to the house. They walked in the garden admiring the flowers. The girls plucked flowers and gave them to the young men.

One girl wandered alone, looking around the garden. She was from Scotland. Suddenly, she saw the thistle near the fence. The thistle was the flower of Scotland. She eagerly asked the young man of the house to bring her a flower.

The young man plucked a flower from the thistle, despite the thorns pricking his fingers. He gave the flower to the girl. She put it in his buttonhole. The two fell in love. It was indeed a proud day for the thistle, who had brought the two together!

37 Ragnard Bolt

Once, a grandson and his grandfather were sitting together. Grandfather was a carver. He had just finished carving the image of Ragnard Bolt with the court of arms. And so, he told his grandson the story of Ragnard Bolt.

Ragnard Bolt dreamt while he slept in a dark cellar of an old castle in Denmark. His long beard had taken root in the marble table upon which he rested. He was a strong soldier of Denmark. Ragnard dreamt of all the good events that would happen in Denmark.

Every Christmas, an angel would visit Ragnard in his dreams. He would confirm that what Ragnard dreamt had actually taken place in Denmark. When Ragnard heard this, he would continue to sleep in peace. Only if Denmark were in danger, he would wake up and strike!

By then, the grandson had fallen asleep and was dreaming of the brave and courageous Ragnard Bolt!

38 The Emperor's New Suit

Once, there was an emperor who was fond of new clothes. He did not care about his kingdom, and kept himself engaged with his wardrobe.

One day, two cheats came to the emperor's kingdom, saying they were the finest weavers in town. They told the emperor that they could produce the most beautiful dress for him. However, the dress could only be seen by the honest and worthy.

The cheats asked for the finest silk, gold threads and money, to set-up their loom. However, they hid all the cloth and pretended to work on invisible lengths of cloth, using the loom.

After some days, the king asked his senior minister to go and check how beautiful the dress looked. The minister went to the loom, but could see no cloth. Yet, the weavers seemed to be working. They asked the minister if he liked the dress. Speechless, the minister agreed with the weavers, as he did not want to look dishonest and unworthy. He told the emperor that the dress was beautiful. The emperor was very pleased to listen to the description!

Finally, the dress was ready and a procession was organised for the public to see the king's new suit. The weavers pretended to dress the emperor in different pieces of clothes, praising them all the time. However, no one, not even the emperor, could see the dress. They all pretended that they could, for no one wanted to look dishonest.

In the procession, nobody could see the emperor's dress, as there was none. But, no one dared to say, as they feared looking unworthy! However, an innocent child from the crowd said, "The emperor has nothing on him!" It was then that everyone, including the emperor, realised their foolishness!

39 The Chief's Ball

A small village was buzzing with excitement. The Chief was holding a ball on the coming Saturday. The evening promised dancing and delicious dinner. All the people in the village had been invited.

John and his family were invited too. John was eager to go to his first ball. He enjoyed dancing and listening to music. He was also looking forward to the grand dinner.

Great preparations were made at the Chief's house. The day before the ball, a number of shiny lights hung from the house. John could hardly sleep the night before the ball.

The next day came bright and sunny. The Chief's house stood whitewashed with ivy hanging down its sides. The guests arrived. The men wore tailcoats and the women were in beautiful gowns.

John danced with the Chief 's daughter. He enjoyed the grand dinner. John returned home satisfied with the evening.

40 The Elves in the Moonlight

Hans was a little boy who lived in a house with a beautiful garden. He played with imaginary fairies and elves. Hans made friends with the bees and other insects who had their homes in the garden.

One day, Hans sat by himself in the moonlit garden. There was a mist hanging in the air. The trees swayed in the gentle breeze. Hans gazed into the distance.

Suddenly, Hans saw tiny green creatures flying near the flower-beds. He cautiously went towards them. He hid behind a tree and watched. The tiny creatures were elves. They were talking among themselves. The elves were waiting for their friends. Hans was excited, but stood quietly.

Once all the elves had arrived, a party began. There was singing, chatting and laughing. Soon, they danced in the moonlight. When it was midnight, all of them disappeared. Hans went to bed, dreaming of the dancing elves.

41 At the Farm

Dorothy and Oliver's parents had sent them to stay at the Dale Farm with a nurse, while they were abroad. The children were elated to be at the farm.

Every morning they would wake up with the crowing of the cock. Then they watched as Mrs. Farmer fed the geese, turkeys, ducks and hens! They went to the stables and teased the drowsy donkeys.

Then, Dorothy and Oliver rode the horse on the soft ground, covered with thistle and grass. In the afternoon, they sat eating sandwiches in the warm sun, and watched little animals play beside them. They had so much fun!

Soon, it was time to return home. Though they were happy to be home after such a long time, the children were sad to leave their new friends at the farm.

However, they both had been such good children that their parents decided to send them again next year!

42 The Ugly Toad

In a deep well, there lived a family of toads. The ugliest toad wished to go out of the well. One day, the ugly toad got into a bucket, which was being used by a farmer to draw water from the well.

The farmer, after drawing the water, saw the ugly toad and exclaimed, "Ugh! You are the ugliest thing I have ever seen!" and threw him away.

The ugly toad then travelled and reached a garden where he met a caterpillar. Suddenly, some fowls came to eat the caterpillar but they saw the ugly toad and flew away. The ugly toad became overconfident that his ugliness could achieve anything.

He then decided to travel to the Sun. One day, the ugly toad hopped on a large kite that he thought would carry him to the Sun. As they flew higher, the ugly toad died of heat, crying sorrowfully over his overconfidence.

43 Not Much!

Once, a young man decided to travel. However, he was never content with anything and kept saying, "Not much, not much."

On his way, he met some fishermen. As they took out the net, the young man said, "Not much fish!" The angry fishermen beat him, thinking he was making fun of them.

A little ahead, the king's men were punishing a thief. Again, the young man said, "Not much punishment!" The king's men heard him and yelled, "You must say, may God pity the poor soul."

A while later, he saw a carpenter polishing furniture. The young man said, "Not much polish!" Furious with his words, the carpenter pushed him. The young man collided with a cart full of people, which fell into a pit. The angry driver of the cart thrashed him, too.

The young man went home and decided not to travel without correcting his habit!

44 The Rude Dwarf

Once there was a gentle lady. She was very kind and helpful.

One day, she was walking in the forest. Just then, she saw a dwarf in trouble. The end of his beard was stuck in a tree. The lady cut his beard to free him. The ungrateful dwarf, instead of thanking her, called her mean for cutting his beard!

Similarly, the lady helped the dwarf three more times, but he always cursed her.

One evening, the lady saw the dwarf again. He had lots of precious stones. The dwarf saw her and screamed rudely. Just then he heard the loud growling of a bear. The frightened dwarf begged the bear to spare him and eat the lady instead. The bear, however, killed the wicked dwarf at once.

Then, the bear changed into a handsome prince. The dwarf had actually tricked him and taken away his treasure. The lady was happily married to the prince.

45 Frankie and Geordie

Once, two friends, Frankie and Geordie lived in a village, close to a forest. The boys' parents always warned them, "Don't go to the forest. The dragon will eat you up!"

However, the two friends loved to play in the forest.

One such day, Frankie and Geordie went deep into the forest. It became dark soon. Just then, they heard a growling sound and soon a scary looking dragon appeared.

Frankie at once climbed the closest tree. However, Geordie still stood on the ground and the dragon moved towards him.

Frankie started throwing branches on the dragon and shouted, "Geordie, run!"

The dragon was confused and Geordie started running. Just then, there were loud sounds in the forest. The villagers had come looking for them! The dragon got scared of the noise, and ran away.

Though the boys were scolded for going into the forest, but Frankie was praised for saving his friend's life.

46 The Son Returns

An old man and his wife were sitting outside their house, remembering their son, who got lost while he was little. Suddenly, a handsome, well-dressed stranger rode up to them.

The old man asked the stranger what he wanted. "A few potatoes the way you eat them, my good man!" he said. The old man asked his wife to prepare a hot potato dish for him.

Then the old man went into the garden to plant saplings. The stranger followed him. He watched the old man tie each sapling firmly to a post. His eyes fell on a crooked tree and he asked, "Did you forget to tie that sapling?"

"Yes. It grew crooked."

"You should have tied me, Father, when I was young," said the stranger. "I would never have run away and got lost."

The old man and his wife wept tears of joy at finding their lost son again.

47 The Thief and the Duke

Once, there was a clever thief. However, a duke had caught him red-handed. The bold thief said, "You are the only person to catch me!"

The duke said, "I will let you go, if you accomplish two tasks. Bring me my horse, and the sheet I sleep under."

The thief disguised himself as a wine-seller. He went to the duke's stables and distributed free drinks. Soon, the grooms fell asleep and he led the horse straight to the duke.

At night, the thief climbed to the duke's bedchamber and hissed at the window. The duke went to the window and the thief pushed him over the ledge. The duchess was scared and ran from the room.

The thief snatched the sheet and escaped. He gave it to the duke the next day. The duke pardoned him. The thief promised that he would be a good man from then on.

48 A Family Reunited

Once, a boy called Hank and his mother lived in the thickest part of the forest. Ten years ago, they were captured by robbers, who had brought them there. They had been living as the robbers' slaves ever since.

Hank had grown up into a strong boy. One day, he asked his mother where their true home was. His mother said, "Our home is in a village. I wish we could escape and go there!"

Hank found a strong branch and hid it. At night, when the robbers were sleeping, Hank hit them on their heads. Then, he stuffed a sack with gold and jewels. Next, he and his mother ran away quickly.

They walked till they came to a pretty cottage in the village. A man stood outside and Hank's mother ran to him. The man recognised his wife and son, and hugged them. The family lived happily ever after.

49 The Goblin's Cave

Rick lived with his mother and father. He was a kind lad.

One day, an old goblin asked Rick for food. He gave him some, but the goblin was greedy, and Rick did not have more food.

The angry goblin snapped his fingers. Suddenly, Rick's hands and feet were tied and he stood inside a cave. Across him, was a beautiful princess, who was also tied.

The wicked goblin captured people who annoyed him and kept them as slaves.

Rick fell in love with the princess and decided to save her and everybody else. He struggled and soon broke open his ropes. When the goblin went out, Rick freed the princess and all the other people.

When the goblin returned, they all pounced on him and tied him with ropes.

Then, Rick took the princess to her father, the king. He was so happy that he married the princess to Rick.

50 The Old Man and the Sisters

Once, there was a woodcutter. One day, he came home empty-handed. He asked his elder daughter to go out and get food.

The elder daughter set out, but lost her way. She came to a house, where an old man lived with his goats. The elder daughter was hungry, so she cooked for herself, ate and slept.

The old man was angry at her selfishness and locked her in the cellar.

The next day, the younger daughter went to look for her sister. She reached the old man's house. There, she cooked food, then fed the old man and his goats. Then, she ate and slept.

The next morning, she woke up in a plush bed. There was a palace where the hut had been.

The old man was actually a handsome, young prince. The kind younger daughter had removed the curse that was on him, so he happily married her.

51 The Story of Corn

God gave man corn to grow as food. Each plant grew hundreds of cobs. Men had plenty of food and they grew careless.

God watched as men paid less and less attention to their food crops. The cornfields grew well and there was lots of corn. Men picked some cobs and left the rest.

One day, a mother and daughter were in the fields. The mother was picking corn. The daughter was playing and fell into a puddle, dirtying her clothes.

The mother, who had washed many clothes that morning, plucked a few cobs and cleaned her daughter's dress using them.

God was furious. "No more corn for you!" he thundered. The number of cobs on each plant decreased.

The men begged for God's mercy. God said, "I am giving you one final chance."

Since then, men have received small amounts of corn, but have always thanked God for their food.

52 The Sledge Ride

Once, there was a boy called Charlie.

Now, Charlie really wanted a sledge. All his friends had one. Even little Toddy Graham boasted about it. Thus, Charlie went to his aunt and requested her to buy him and his sister, Molly, a sledge. However, his aunt refused and asked him to play with his other toys instead.

This annoyed Charlie. Thus, he took one of his aunt's new tea-trays to use as a sledge.

Charlie and Molly's first ride downhill was a success; but on the second one, Charlie could not steer it properly, and — Wham! They crashed into Toddy Graham's sledge. Their aunt's tray crashed into pieces. Poor Molly was hurt! Charlie felt very guilty, and took care of his sister. He saved his pocket money and bought his aunt a new tray. Aunt gifted both of them a sledge on Christmas. They understood why she had refused to get it earlier!

53 The Lost Nest

Once, a family of birds lived in the forest. The parent birds would go looking for food for themselves and their babies every day.

One day, when the parent birds were away to look for food, a hailstorm occurred. The heavy rain and strong wind caused their nest to blow away and land on the branch of a tree far away.

When the mother bird returned, she could not find her nest. She tried to look for it in vain. She called out to the father bird and sobbed, "I cannot find our nest!"

He tried to comfort her and began searching.

They searched the place where their tree stood, but were unable to locate it. Thus, they decided to look further away and flew high. After searching for a long time, they found their nest on another tree. They saw that the babies were safe. Happily, they hugged them!

54 The Boy Who Became a Robin

According to Raghu's family tradition, every young lad had to go on a long fast to have a guardian angel. The time had come for Raghu, a young Indian boy, to meet his angel.

Raghu's father was very religious, and wanted his son to have the best guardian angel. Hence, he asked Raghu to fast for twelve days.

Fasting for twelve days was difficult for Raghu. On the last few days, he begged his father to let him eat, as he feared he would die of hunger. However, his father insisted that he carry on. On the twelfth day, the father went to his son with food, but by then, Raghu was already talking to his guardian angel, who had decided to punish the cruel father.

As a punishment to his father, the guardian angel turned Raghu into a robin forever, to sing sweet songs far away from his father.

55 Tom's Friends

Once, there was a boy called Tom. He lived with his parents. Poor Tom was very shy and so he did not have any friends.

Then, one day, Aunt Gertrude came to meet him. He loved his aunt greatly, so he told her how he wanted to play with the boys in the neighbourhood, but was scared to join them.

The next day, Aunt Gertrude went with Tom to the neighbourhood. There she started calling out to children to come and play ball with them. Soon, a lot of boys came forward and started playing.

Now, every day, the boys would get together in the afternoons and play till tea-time. Aunt Gertrude called them 'The Scratch Team.'

Tom was very happy. He had friends now. Most of them even went to the same school as him. Tom thanked Aunt Gertrude, for she had helped him make good friends!

56 The Water Spirit

Once, a farmer was working on his farm. Suddenly, the wicked Water Spirit of the well appeared before him. She said, "I will give you plenty of riches, if you will give me what was born in your house today."

The farmer agreed blindly. However, when he returned home, he was shocked to hear that his wife had had a baby boy!

The farmer kept quiet about his promise to the Water Spirit. He was frightened and moved to another town. The boy was kept away from wells, and the farmer grew richer and richer! Soon, the boy turned into a fine young man. He was engaged by the Count to be his official hunter.

One day, while hunting a deer, the man went near the Water Spirit's well. He stretched out his hand for water, and the Water Spirit recognised him and pulled him in.

The man's mother was upset that her husband had promised the Water Spirit their son. She asked a wise old woman what she could do to save her son. The woman gave her a golden spinning wheel and a thistle. She told her to spin on a full moon night and sleep by the well. If the Water Spirit appeared, she was to throw the thistle at her feet.

The woman did what she was told and when she had spun lots of thread, she went to sleep. After a while, her son emerged from the well. He pulled himself up by the thread. Screaming with anger, the Water Spirit followed.

The mother quickly threw the thistle at the Water Spirit's feet. It sprang into a huge, prickly bush and the Water Spirit howled in pain. She could not move as she was stuck! The mother and her son ran far away to safety.

57 Fishing at the Pool

Once, a boy called Ron lived with his brother Frank and their parents.

One day, Frank decided to go fishing. When the boys reached the pool, Frank started fishing. Ron sat waiting for Frank, for he did not like fishing.

So he lay down next to the stream. He moved closer to the water and noticed many fish grouped together, talking about something. One very small fish wanted to taste the worm on Frank's bait, but his mother forbade him. Ron wanted to tell the little fish that his mother was right!

He woke up with a start, and saw an excited Frank winding his chord. He realised that the little fish was caught by the bait.

Just then, Frank slipped, and fell on the ground and lost the little fish in the water. Ron felt sorry for Frank, but was glad that the little fish was now safe!

58 Philip at the Party

Philip was a young man. He was a cheerful, handsome and a kind man. Everybody had a good word to say about Philip.

Once, Philip had to attend a party in the evening. The people were looking forward to a delicious dinner and merry dancing.

At the party, Philip was standing in the corner and tapping his foot to the music. Suddenly, he spotted the prettiest girl in the room. He watched her dancing gaily.

Philip was charmed by the beautiful girl. He walked up to her and asked her for a dance. They danced together the entire evening. All eyes in the room followed the couple.

Philip had never enjoyed dancing so much with anyone. He wanted to dance for a long time with the charming girl.

Philip then asked the girl to marry him. The girl smiled and said, "Yes." Thereafter, Philip and the girl were happily married.

59 The Wonderful Son

Once, there lived a boy called George.

One night, George's father had gone out for some work. George's mother had very high fever. Thus, he at once left home and ran to bring the doctor. Suddenly, it started raining heavily. The night was very dark and George was wet and cold. While running down the hill, he fell and hurt his head on a stone.

Poor George was so hurt that he fainted. While returning home, his father found George lying on the ground and took him to the doctor. When George woke up, he asked the doctor to go and check on his mother.

Thus, George, with a bandage on his head, his father and the doctor went in a carriage to his home. There, the doctor gave his mother some medicine and she was better soon. George's parents were very happy to have such a wonderful son!

60 The Bathtub Sailor

There was a doll that wore trousers and a sailor's cap. He had broken his neck, in an attempt to jump off the table, and was put away in the drawer.

He was a proud doll, who thought he was no less than a human, as he had arms and legs, eyes and mouth. He remembered how children would put him in his boat and he would sail in the bathtub, and sighed.

Then, one day, someone opened the drawer and picked him up. "This doll will be fine. I will stitch his neck." A needle poked his neck and stitched him up. He felt as good as new!

Then, a boy's small hand clutched him tightly and he looked up. "You are a sailor," said the boy to him, "so you shall sail."

The boy placed him in a boat and patted him encouragingly. Both played happily for hours.

61 The Trusting Wife

Once, an old man lived with his wife in a small hut. They were poor but loved each other a lot. One day, the wife sent him to sell their cow in the market for some money. The man went with his friend.

There, he sold the cow in exchange for a colourful parrot. His friend warned, "Your wife needed money. She will be very angry with you."

The man replied, "She always agrees with what I do. I bet she will like the parrot."

The friend was not convinced and promised him hundred gold coins if his wife did not scold him.

After they reached home, the wife saw the parrot and said, "My husband always takes the right decision. I am sure whatever he did is good for us."

The friend was amazed and gave the man hundred gold coins. The man and his wife were very happy.

62 The Little Bird Angel

Once, there lived a boy called Hans. He could not walk as he did not have feet.

Hans had a beautiful little bird, which sang him melodious songs. One day, while he was sitting in his room reading a book, a wicked cat entered the room and sat staring at the bird. Hans knew that the cat wanted to eat his bird and screamed at it, but the cat would not move. So, Hans threw the book at the cat, but she escaped and jumped to reach the cage. The cage fell down and the bird inside fluttered helplessly.

Hans did not think about himself and jumped out of his chair. Though he fell hard, he picked up the cage.

The bird was actually Hans' angel. Seeing Hans' selflessness, it gave him a pair of golden feet to reward his golden heart. Kind Hans could walk and run now!

63 The Pond Newspaper

Once, some fish lived in a pond.

One day, the fish decided to start a newspaper for themselves, like the one humans read. It would provide them with information about the Pond Kingdom.

The writers for the newspaper had been selected. However, there was great confusion while deciding the writer for the 'Jokes' section.

All the fish wanted someone funny to be the writer of the 'Jokes' section.

Then, the goldfish had an idea. He said, "Let us make the frog the writer! He looks funny and has a funny voice! He is the funniest creature, since he lives on both land and water. He is a half fish!"

All the fish started laughing at the goldfish's idea. Another fish said, "The very thought of the frog makes us laugh! He should indeed be the joke writer!"

Thus, the frog was made the joke writer and the newspaper was named 'Croak'.

64 The Three Brothers

Once, three young men, who were sons of farmers, wanted to make a lot of money quickly. So, they decided to trade with other lands and become rich.

They took all their money and travelled from place to place. They were able to make some money, but spent more money than they earned. After three years, they realised they had very little money left.

As a last try, they bought a lot of fine, woven cloth and started going from town to town, trying to sell it. Many other traders were also selling good cloth at the same time. Thus, they could sell only a little cloth and suffered a huge loss.

As they travelled back home, they thought, "Maybe if we had stayed home, we would have been better off. At least we know how to farm. We could have eaten well and lived in our own house."

65 The Humble Artist

Once, an artist lived in the ancient city of Rome. He made very beautiful paintings. However, he was not confident about his work and felt that people would not appreciate it. So, he never tried to sell his paintings and lived in poverty.

One day, a woman came to his place to get her portrait made. She was extremely beautiful. The artist was struck by her beauty and agreed. He painted her portrait in a week. When the woman saw it, she was very happy. She gave the artist good money and encouraged him to sell his paintings.

The artist finally agreed and sold them. People gave large sums of money in return and he became rich and popular.

After sometime, he went to the woman and thanked her. She said, "You were brilliant at your work but lacked confidence. Now you have it."

Later, they both got married and lived happily.

66 The Right Decision

One day, an old man decided to sell his horse. His wife agreed and he set off. On the way, the old man met someone who had two apples and exchanged the horse for it.

On his way back, he met two gentlemen who were carrying two sacks. The old man stopped to talk to them. They were curious about the apples that he was holding in his hands.

Hearing the entire story, the gentlemen said, "If your wife doesn't scold you for bringing two apples for a horse, we will give you a sack full of money." The old man agreed.

Then they all went to the old man's home. There, the wife saw the two apples in the man's hands. She happily said, "Just what our neighbours wanted! They are foreigners and do not get apples in their home country! We shall sell these to them now! You are always right!"

The gentlemen gave them money as promised. The old couple also sold the two apples to their foreigner neighbours and lived comfortably from then on.

67 Tears of a Princess

Once, there was a king who had three daughters.

One day, the king asked his daughters, "How much do you love me?" The elder daughters said that they loved him the most in the world. However, his youngest daughter answered, "Without salt, food is tasteless. I love my father like salt." The king was furious and banished her.

The youngest daughter wept tears of pearls as she left and was never heard of again.

Many years later, the king sent one of his counts to the forest for hunting. There, he met an old woman, carrying a heavy load. The kind count carried the woman's heavy load to her house. There, he met her ugly daughter. The daughter looked at him and went out to mind the geese.

The old woman gave him a little box with a single pearl inside, as a gift.

The count later went to the royal court. He remembered the gift and gave it to the queen. She opened the box and fainted. When she recovered, she told him that the pearl was exactly like the ones her daughter had wept, so many years ago.

The count promised he would look for the old woman. When he reached the old woman's house, he climbed a tree to watch. After a while, he heard sounds. He looked around and saw the ugly daughter take off her ugly skin. Lo and behold, she transformed into a beautiful girl with golden hair! The count was so surprised that he fell off the branch, and landed near the daughter's feet!

He got on his horse and rode to the palace, without stopping.

He brought the king and queen back. The king and queen embraced their daughter and thanked the old woman for looking after her. The count was rewarded handsomely, by the king, for reuniting them.

68 Derek and Joy

Derek lived on a farm with his parents. He went to a school across the countryside. The long journey to and from school was boring as well as tiring.

One day, Derek decided to take his goat, Joy, along. He had great fun with Joy on the way.

On reaching school, Derek tied Joy under a tree and headed for his class.

Poor Joy, he had never been tied up before. He bleated as loudly as he could, but to no avail. Thirsty and hungry, he started chewing his rope.

Suddenly, Joy was free! He trotted towards Derek's class. He saw Derek seated near a window, put his head inside and nearly chewed off Derek's hair in happiness.

The children rolled with laughter. Even the teacher could not stop laughing.

Derek was embarrassed. He vowed never to take Joy to school again. He decided to travel with his guinea pig the next day!

69 Cheerful Rasmus

Once, there lived a boy called Rasmus. His mother worked as a nursemaid at a manor. She was kind and believed in God. His father was a tailor. However, he fell very ill and died.

Rasmus and his mother became poor. Rasmus decided to go on a tour around the world to learn. However, people cheated him and he returned home a very sad person, with no hopes from life. He never tried to improve his life, for he thought no good would come of it.

Then one day, under the willow tree, Rasmus met John. Soon they became friends. John read out psalms for Rasmus. Slowly, Rasmus started believing in the mercy of God.

Quite soon, Rasmus became a cheerful young man. He started working on a farm. He faced problems sometimes, but then he believed that God would help him through them. And so, he was always happy.

70 A Son's Prayers

One day, a little boy was very sad. The boy's mother was terribly ill. He loved her dearly. She played with him, and read him stories. The little boy wanted her to recover soon.

The little boy remembered a story his mother had told him. In the story, a little boy had scraped the rust from the church bell so his mother would recover from an illness. He decided he would do the same, hoping his mother would get well.

The boy went to the church in the middle of the night. He climbed up to the bell tower. He was very sacred but scraped the rust from the bell.

The boy came down crying from the bell tower. The minister found him in this condition.

The minister found out why the boy was unhappy. Together, they prayed for the boy's mother. The little boy's mother was better by the morning.

71 The Ass' Cruel Master

Once, there was a hard-working ass. But his master did not treat him well.

One day, his master loaded him with a huge load of earthenware.

The ass did not have much strength. The road on which he had to carry the load was uneven and rough. This was very difficult for the ass. He kept slipping many times.

Suddenly, the ass lost his balance and fell down on the ground. All the earthen vessels broke into many pieces.

His master was very angry, as now he would not be able to earn any money. He began to beat the ass without any pity.

The ass, feeling much pain in his heart and body, lifted his head from the ground and sternly said, "You selfish, greedy and cruel man. You first starve me by giving little food, and then load me with more than I can carry; you deserve this bad luck because of your injustice to me."

72 The Guard Dogs

Once, there lived a young boy. The boy had a special gift. He could understand the language of dogs and could talk to them.

One day, the boy came to know that far away in a kingdom, the people were being troubled by a pack of dogs that ate little children at night. The king had declared a huge reward for anyone who could solve the problem.

The boy at once set off for the kingdom, where he met the king. After listening to the lad, the king asked his men to escort the boy to the place where the dogs hovered.

After sometime, the boy returned to the palace and informed the king that the dogs were under a spell. They were guarding a treasure, which was buried in the forest.

The hidden treasure was taken out and distributed among the people. The dogs mysteriously disappeared and never returned.

73 The Fortune-teller

Once, there lived a lady, who was a fortune-teller. She lived in a small hut. She told people their future in exchange of gold.

The lady used all kinds of tricks to convince people. People believed whatever she told them. Soon, she became famous and rich. She bought a new house and rented out her old hut to another poor woman.

Out of habit, people continued to go to the old hut. The new lady told them that she was not a fortune-teller. However, people did not believe her. She had no option but to tell people what they wanted to hear from her. Thus, many people started to come to her.

Thereafter, the lady who first lived there became poor, because no one went to her now.

Thus, the old hut changed the fate of its new mistress and the old mistress lost her trade.

74 The Jumper

Once, there was a city in the mountains called Hope Land. The king of Hope Land wanted to find a match for his daughter, the princess. Thus, he invited all the suitors to his palace and said, "Whoever jumps the highest will be married to my daughter, for he will be the bravest man of Hope Land."

Many suitors came forward to win the hand of the beautiful princess. However, no one could jump high. In the end, three suitors entered the palace - a flea, a grasshopper and Jack, the toy.

First, the flea came forward. He said, "I have royal blood in my veins. I have good manners, and so I am fit to marry the princess and become the future king!" Then, he jumped. He rose a few feet in the air but, at that moment, the chambermaid waved the king's fan. The wind from the fan blew the flea away!

Next, the grasshopper came forward. He said, "I belong to an ancient Egyptian family. We are well-mannered, learned and royal. Thus, I should get the princess' hand." Then, he jumped. However, his foot slipped as he jumped and he fell on the king's face.

This made the king very angry. He ordered his guards to throw the grasshopper out of the palace.

Now it was Jack, the toy's turn. He did not say anything, but prepared to jump. He jumped very high, and then landed straight in front of the princess.

The king was very happy now. He said, "Jack the toy did not talk like the flea and the grasshopper, but jumped the highest. He does not boast about himself, but believes in his work. He shall marry my daughter!"

Soon, Jack, the toy was married to the princess, and they lived happily.

75 A Storm in the Sea

Once, there lived a poor boy. His parents died in an accident and there was no one to look after him.

The boy often sat on the seashore and drew on sand. This way, the boy grew up to be a good artist.

One day, the boy found a magic paintbrush. Anything he painted turned into reality! Thus, he helped people with food and clothes.

One day, the king heard about the magic paintbrush and the painter. He asked him to paint an island of gold.

So, the painter painted a sea and an island in gold in the middle. As soon as the painting was complete, it turned real.

The king started sailing towards the golden island. Then, the painter painted a deadly storm in the sea. The king drowned in the storm and died. The painter felt very bad and he threw the paintbrush in the sea.

76 The Son's Bravery

Once, there lived a rich man who had a son. The son was very foolish and could not learn anything. The rich man sent him to three different masters for a year. When he came back, the boy's father asked him what he had learnt.

The boy said, "I have learnt the language of the dogs, the frogs and the birds." Hearing this, the rich man was very angry and told his son to leave his house.

The boy left home and went to another kingdom. There, a witch had kidnapped the baby prince. The boy at once offered his help in finding the prince. The brave boy went alone into the jungle. With the help of his knowledge of talking to animals; he found where the baby prince was and saved him. The king rewarded the boy for his bravery and appointed him as a minister in the court.

77 Loyal Oscar

Once, a man brought a dog and named him Oscar. However, the man's wife did not like Oscar.

Oscar's master trained him to bring his mid-day meal from home.

One day, the master's wife made mutton for her husband. She hung the lunch box around Oscar's neck and sent him to the fields.

On the way, Oscar met a bigger dog. The bigger dog asked Oscar for the meat but Oscar refused.

The bigger dog tried to snatch the box from him. They fought and Oscar was injured.

The master's friend saw the two dogs fighting and recognised Oscar. He hit the bigger dog with a stick and drove him away.

Now, he carried the dog to his master and told him the entire story. The master had tears in his eyes. He bandaged the dog and took him home. Even the master's wife was ashamed and praised the dog for his loyalty.

78 Joy and Sorrow

Every morning, the fishermen went to the sea to catch fish and other sea animals. Then they would sell them in the market and earn money.

One day, the fishermen went to the sea with their big net. They threw the net in the water. When it was time to pull up the net, they all became very happy as it was very heavy. As they pulled the net, they were all very disappointed. The net was full of sand and stones and the fish were very few. It was not what they had expected.

An old and wise fisherman said, "We should all stop crying about it. The truth is that sorrow is the sister of happiness. At one moment we were very happy and the next moment we were sad. If we accept the joys of life, we should suffer the pain also. We should learn from it."

79 Edward's Canary

Once, there were two brothers, Raymond and Edward. Both of them had a pet each. Raymond had a cat and Edward a canary. Surprisingly, the cat and the canary were also good friends. However, Edward never trusted the cat.

One day, Edward was playing in a park near their house. Suddenly, he saw the cat running towards him followed by Tim, his little brother. The cat had the canary in his mouth. Edward was upset and angry.

He thought, 'Oh! The cat ate my canary!'

Edward picked up a stick and hit the cat hard on its head.

"What have you done?" exclaimed Tim. "The canary was hurt, that's why the cat carried it to you."

Edward was ashamed. He thought, "I should have trusted the cat."

Edward took care of both the cat and the canary. He promised himself that, henceforth, he would always think before reacting to anything.

80 The Magic Carpet and Cloak

Once, a lady set out to free her husband who was under the spell of an evil witch. The evil witch had transformed him into a mouse and was holding him captive in her castle.

The lady did not know the location of the witch's castle. She asked the Sun for directions to the castle. The Sun could not help her, but gave her a basket to use whenever she was in trouble. The basket contained a magic carpet that could take a person anywhere.

The lady then asked the Moon to help her. The Moon gave her a magic cloak and sent her to the wind.

The wind told her the location of the castle and gave her a magic potion to transform her husband. The lady reached the castle in the magic cloak. She gave her husband the magic potion and they flew back home on the carpet.

81 The Wicked Maid

Once, there lived a beautiful princess. She set out on a journey to marry a prince from a neighbouring kingdom. Her maid and her horse accompanied the princess. This horse was a talking horse and was extremely loyal to the princess.

While in the forest, the maid imprisoned the princess and dressed as the princess herself. The maid made the princess promise not to reveal her true identity.

The talking horse saw all that happened, but it kept quiet fearing for the princess' life. Now, the maid did not know that the horse could talk. She was sure that her plan to marry the prince would succeed.

They reached the prince's kingdom. Everyone thought that the maid was the princess. But the talking horse told the prince the truth. The princess was recognised by her royal seal. The prince and princess were married. The wicked maid was punished.

82 The Helpful Boy

Once, there was a boy who lived in a village. Everyone liked him because he was very helpful and caring.

One day, when he was going to school, he saw an old woman crossing the road. He went to help the woman but, while doing so, he fell on a pile of logs and broke his ankle.

The doctor plastered his ankle and advised him six weeks' rest. He was very sad because he could not go to school, and he had to appear for his examinations the next month.

The boy asked his best friend to come to his house and explain the lessons, but his friend refused saying that he had to study himself. He asked his other friends but they too gave some excuse. At last, his teachers helped him in preparing for the examination.

The helpful boy scored the highest marks in his class!

83 Jack and his Puppy

Once, there was a boy called Jack who loved horses. On Jack's birthday, his father got him a puppy. Jack was very unhappy. He said, "Father, I want a pony!"

His father said, "Son, you are too young to have a pony. Take good care of the puppy and I will get you a pony, once you are a little older."

Feeling sad, Jack left his house and started walking towards the nearby forest. He was so gloomy that he did not see a ditch in the forest and fell in it.

Jack started shouting and crying, loudly. Now, the puppy had followed Jack to the forest. When he saw Jack fall, he ran home and started yelping before Jack's father. The father understood that something was wrong. He followed the puppy to the forest and pulled Jack out of the ditch.

Jack understood that his puppy had saved him. He happily hugged the puppy!

84 Following Instructions

Once, there lived a man called Hans. One day, his wife Gretel said, "Hans, my mother is coming to our house for supper tonight. Please take a paper bag, a jute bag and a glass bottle to the market place. Buy some olives and put them in this paper bag. Then, buy some ice and put it in the jute bag. Finally, buy some honey and put it in this bottle."

Hans went to the market place. The vegetable shop's owner said, "Sir, I do not have olives, but I have olive juice!" Thus, Hans bought olive juice and put it in the paper bag.

Next, Hans went to buy ice. The shopkeeper said, "Sir, I do not have ice, but I have cold water!" Hans bought cold water and put it in the jute bag.

Now, Hans went to buy honey. The shopkeeper said, "Sir, I do not have honey, but I have a beehive that you can take!" Hans bought a beehive, but as he tried to stuff the beehive in the glass bottle, the angry honeybees stung him on his face and hands.

Stung and crying, Hans reached home. Gretel said, "Oh, Hans! What happened to you? The paper bag, the jute bag and the bottle are all empty!"

Hans told Gretel about the events of the market place. Gretel said, "Foolish Hans! You put juice in the paper bag, and it leaked! You put water in the jute bag, and that leaked too! You should never meddle with a beehive that is why the bees stung you! Now you are hurt. All your money is wasted and you returned from the market empty handed!"

Hans said, "You are right. Now I will always use my mind, not just follow instructions, blindly."

85 A New Member

In a clear blue ocean, there lived many little fish. This school of fish lived a carefree life, doing as they pleased. Unknown to all dangers, they swam together in a group.

One day, they heard a huge crashing sound in the ocean. All the underwater creatures went to investigate the newest member of the ocean. They thought it was an enemy and went to fight it. But the dolphin advised them to stay away from it, lest it caught them. However, some brave sea folk went closer to inspect, and they saw a human figure. And then to their greatest disbelief, they saw that its lower body was a fish's tail. The wise octopus then told everyone that this mystical creature was a mermaid.

The mermaid begged, "Please allow me to stay here, I will not do any harm to your beautiful sea."

All the creatures welcomed the gentle mermaid lovingly.

86 The Proud Donkey

One day, a traveller went on a journey. He loaded one donkey with a sack of money and the other with a sack of grains and left.

The donkey that had the sack of money on him walked with his head held high. He was very proud to carry money on his back. He walked so fast that the bell around his neck rang loudly and clearly. The second donkey that was carrying grains walked behind the first donkey quietly.

When the traveller and his donkeys reached a lonely road, many robbers jumped out from the bushes. The traveller tried to fight with them. But the robbers wounded the donkey that was carrying the money and stole the money sack.

The donkey that was carrying the grains was left unhurt. He saw the wounded donkey and said, "Friend, you should not have been haughty and made all this noise."

87 The Boy Who Couldn't Shudder

Once a dim-witted young man heard his brother say, "I can do everything but tasks that give a shudder." His brother was referring to frightening tasks.

Since then, the young man always said, "If only I could shudder!" People helped him, thinking it was easy to frighten someone.

First came the priest, dressed up as a ghost. The young man was not scared. He thought the ghost was a robber and pushed him from the church building. Alas! The priest broke his leg but the young man uttered, "If only I could shudder!"

On somebody's advice, the young man stayed at a place where seven hanging bodies shook in the wind. He thought they must be cold; so he set up a fire. The young man was annoyed when their clothing caught fire and hung them back! He uttered, "If only I could shudder!"

A king challenged him that he had to stay in a haunted castle for three days. If he was not scared, he would marry the princess. On the first day, there were wild cats and dogs that tried to haunt him. But he cut them into pieces.

The second day, he encountered skeletons but our young man played with the skulls.

The third day, he came across a coffin. He cuddled with the dead body to make it warm. When the dead body was revived, it tried to kill the young man. But he locked it back in the coffin and uttered, "If only I could shudder!"

The king married the young man to the princess.

One day, the princess brought icy water and splashed it on the young man as he slept. He immediately awoke, trembling; "Now I know what it means to shudder!"

However, the young man never understood what it meant to shudder in fear!

88 Little Thumbling

Once, there lived a carpenter and his wife. They had everything but were sad, as they did not have any children. God listened to their prayers and blessed them with a child but it was only as big as a thumb. So they named him Thumbling.

The parents loved their child. One day, the carpenter was going to the forest to cut wood. He wanted his wife to come in the afternoon and help him. Before leaving, the wife asked Thumbling to look after the house.

When everybody was asleep, two thieves entered the carpenter's house. Little Thumbling was surprised to see the thieves steal valuables and grains.

Thumbling quietly ran to the neighbour's house and told him about the thieves. The neighbour called some friends and came to the carpenter's house. The thieves started running but everybody followed them and beat them badly. Everybody was very proud of Thumbling.

89 The Magical Pear

One day, an old man was selling pears. He came near the house of a poor couple.

The old lady who was standing in the porch saw his tired face and offered him a glass of water. Grateful for her kindness, the old pear seller came in to drink water. He was indeed very thirsty.

While leaving, he handed a pear to the old couple. He asked them to share the pear and their dream would be fulfilled. The poor couple did not believe in magic, but the pear looked so delicious that they shared it.

The next day, while they were talking, they realised that both had the same dream the previous night. Both had dreamed of living in a huge house.

Later that day, when the old lady's husband was ploughing his garden, he found a metal chest full of gold coins. The pear seller's words had come true.

90 The Special Puppy

Once, a farmer wanted to sell puppies.

A little boy went to the farmer and said, "Sir, can I buy one of your puppies?"

The farmer said, "Of course! But it will cost lots of money."

Now the boy had very little money, so he said, "Can I just see them?"

The farmer whistled and the puppies came running out. The last one was limping.

"What is wrong with him?" asked the little boy.

The farmer said, "He has injured one leg. He cannot run and play."

The little boy's eyes lit up. He sat down and rolled up his pants. He had steel braces and a special shoe. He said, "I can't run and play either. We will understand each other."

The farmer said, "You may have him for free. He will be your best friend. I am glad he's got you."

The little boy walked home happily with his puppy.

112

91 The Kind Ferryman

Diogenes was a great thinker who lived in Greece. He had a sharp mind, so many people respected him.

Once, during his travels, Diogenes found himself before a stream in flood. He could not cross over. The stream flowed swiftly by, carrying branches and stones. Diogenes watched helplessly.

The kind ferryman, who often rowed people across the stream in his boat, saw Diogenes. "Come!" said the ferryman, "I will row you safely across!"

Diogenes was very thankful. The kind ferryman told him, "You don't need to pay me."

Just then the ferryman saw an angry and mean traveller. The ferryman rowed his boat to help him, too.

Seeing this, Diogenes said, "Now I can see that you are not really a kind and good man. Helping people is just a habit for you!"

The ferryman was shocked and hurt to hear Diogenes. He understood that not everybody understands kindness.

92 Hard Work

Long ago, Jupiter wanted to rent out his farm. So he sent Mercury to advertise for the farm.

Farmers from everywhere gathered together at the market-place to hear the announcement.

The farmers thought that it was too expensive. Then one bold farmer from the crowd decided to hire the farm. The deal was closed between Jupiter and the farmer.

Now whatever the farmer planted grew well. Be it the cold of winter or the heat of summer or the rains, that year the farmer had a good harvest. Even his neighbours were surprised at the yield.

This made the farmer proud and lazy. But the next year, the weather changed and all he planted was in vain. Then the farmer realised that without hard work, the results will never be good. He would only get divine blessings after putting in hard work.

93 The Bald Men and the Comb

It was a beautiful evening. A bald man went out for a walk, enjoying the cool breeze.

Suddenly something on the ground struck his foot. It was a comb!

Just as he bent down to pick it up, a stranger called out to him, "I saw it, too! We must share it!"

The bald man smiled, "Of course, I will share it with you, but I do not think it will help you at all!" Then, the bald man opened his palm to show the stranger the comb.

The stranger silently looked at the comb. He could not use it, for he too was bald.

The bald man said, "The gods wanted to give us something good, but Fate did not want the gift to be useful. Instead of giving us hair, he gave us a round moon on our heads."

He threw the comb and walked back home.

94 A Tiger for a Pet

Once there was a little boy called Harry. He loved tigers. He had tiger toys, posters and blankets and watched tiger videos.

As Harry's birthday drew near, he asked his parents to gift him a tiger.

On the day of his birthday, Harry received a hat from his grandparents, a pair of socks from his uncle but did not receive any gift from his parents. He was hurt and started crying bitterly. Then, his father took him to the garage and showed him a big box. Inside the box was a tiger. Harry hugged the tiger in joy. The tiger, in turn, licked his face.

The same day Harry bought a collar for the tiger so that he could take him out for a walk.

That evening Harry took the tiger to the park for a walk. He wanted to show the tiger to all his friends. But, all his friends got scared and ran away on seeing the tiger.

The next day, Harry took the tiger to school. The same thing happened there and everyone jumped out of the classroom, including the teacher who had taught them about tigers.

Harry thought that his dear granny would be pleased to see the tiger, but she too screamed and ran away on seeing it.

Harry came back home upset and told his father about the problem.

Harry's father immediately made a call. In a few minutes, a man came with a big lorry and took the tiger back to Africa. Then, Harry and his father went to a pet shop and picked up a cute little puppy.

Everyone liked the little puppy. Harry's granny even gave him dog food, every time he visited her.

Since then, every summer, Harry and his family went to Africa to visit the tigers.

95 Gold Coins

Once, there lived a peasant. He worked hard, but still could not earn enough to take care of his family.

The peasant had an ass, which he used to carry wood from the forest.

One day, the peasant fell ill. Whatever little money he had, was spent on his treatment. The peasant's wife wanted to sell the ass, but the peasant did not allow that.

The peasant's wife prayed for her husband's good health and happiness. That night while going to sleep, she saw a bright light appear in front of her. Then she heard a voice say, "Your ass is extraordinary. If you pat him thrice on his back, he spits out gold coins."

The wife immediately tried it out and the ass spit out gold coins.

Soon, the peasant was well again. He became very rich and took good care of his family. They all lived happily.

96 Lessons for Life

Once, a young man requested a trainer to teach him the art of sword fighting.

The trainer agreed. Now, the young man started living in the trainer's house.

The next day onwards, the trainer made the young man get up early in the morning. He then made him do all the daily chores like washing, cleaning and cooking. Later in the afternoon, the young man would take the trainer's sheep to graze. Then in the evening he would chop wood for the fire.

One day, the young man got fed up and said, "I have come here to learn and not do household work. Kindly begin my lessons."

The trainer laughed and said, "Young man, these are life's lessons. You have learned to live independently. Also, you have developed the stamina to face any circumstances in life."

The young man understood and thanked his trainer for the lessons.

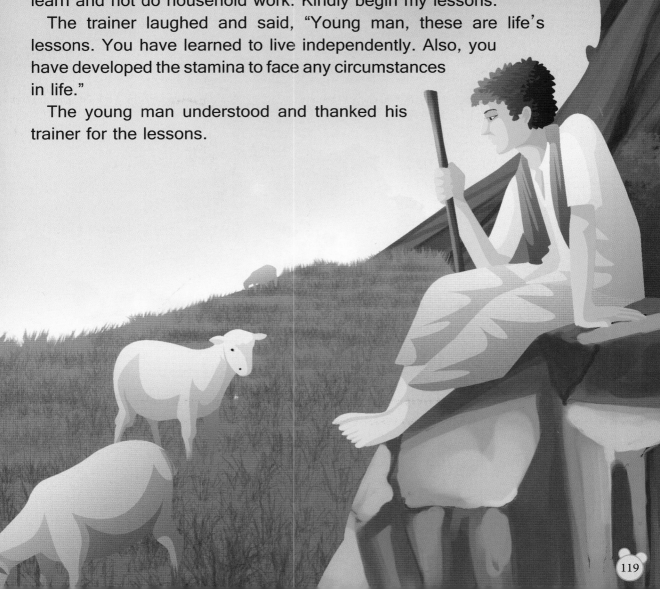

97 Dog Saves the Lion

One day, a lion was hunting in the forest. Just then, he heard the sound of horses galloping towards him. The lion understood that hunters were coming after him. He started running.

Sadly, the hunters caught him and flung a net on him.

The hunters were very hungry. Thus, they tied the lion's net to a tree and sat down to eat. Soon, they all fell asleep under the nearby trees.

The hunters had also fed the dogs. One of the hunters' dogs was very kind. He offered the lion some food. The lion cried out, "Oh! How can I eat? My poor family will be hungry and waiting for me!"

The dog felt very sad for the lion. He tried to cut the ropes and the net with his teeth. The lion tried too and soon he was free! He thanked the dog and ran off to his family.

98 A Lesson in Humility

Once, there lived a proud man with his wife. The man used to drive the chariot of the king.

One day, he said to his wife, "You must come and see me, then you will feel proud of me."

The wife went to see her husband drive the king's chariot. She noticed that he was driving the chariot very arrogantly, whereas the king sat in his chariot calm and composed.

In the evening, when the man returned, his wife said, "I want to leave you."

"Leave me!" exclaimed the man, "You want to leave the king's chariot driver! You are very foolish."

The wife replied to her proud husband, "I came to see you drive the king today. He is the king, yet he is so modest and humble. You are just his driver but you are so arrogant."

The man was very ashamed and became humble from then on.

99 The Miserly Merchant

Once there was a wealthy, miserly merchant. He wore an old torn pair of slippers.

One day, the merchant visited a public bath and left his slippers outside. On his return he found new slippers there. Thinking that they were a gift, he wore them.

The new slippers belonged to a judge. The merchant was called to the court and was punished for stealing them.

The merchant threw his old slippers out of the window. They fell into a fisherman's net and damaged it. The angry fisherman threw them back and broke the merchant's expensive vase.

Now, the merchant was fed up with his slippers and decided to bury them. However, a neighbour thought that he was burying guns and complained about him. He was called to the court again. In tears, he told the judge the entire story. The kind judge told him that he should not be miserly.

100 Chuck and the Ship-builders

One day, there was a young boy called Chuck. Everyone in the village knew that Chuck was a good storyteller

One day, Chuck passed by a ship-builder's workshop. The ship-builders requested him for a story. Chuck was silent.

Then, a ship-builder said, "Chuck, we are the mightiest of all on Earth! Everybody else should listen to what we say and do what we ask!"

These words annoyed Chuck. He said, "I know a good story…Before the Earth was made, God made Chaos and Water. God then decided to make Mother Earth. So, he made Earth and asked her to swallow the sea. In the first gulp, the mountains came up. In the second gulp, the plains came up, flat and dry. Earth has not taken a third gulp — if she did, there would be no water and no ship-builders or ships! So be grateful to God!"

101 The Philosopher among the Tombs

Once upon a time, there lived a philosopher. He was intelligent and knowledgeable.

One day, he went to a graveyard. He found two human skeletons, one was of a duke and the other of a common beggar.

The philosopher looked closely at both the skeletons and could not make out the difference between the two. Their bones looked the same.

After spending some time in reasoning he said, "If the body structure of all human beings is made in the same form, then surely the way a man behaves depends on the mind and not the blood and bones."

God made us all equal when he created us. Human beings differentiate on the basis of skin colour, blood and religion. When we die, we all become the same sand. Then no one can differentiate what we were, which religions we belonged to, or from where we came.

OTHER TITLES IN THIS SERIES

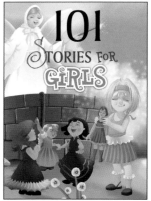

ISBN: 978-93-80069-62-3

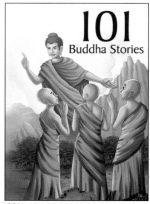

ISBN: 978-93-80069-58-6

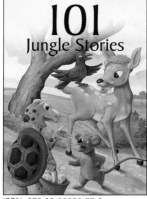

ISBN: 978-93-80069-57-9

ISBN: 978-93-80069-59-3

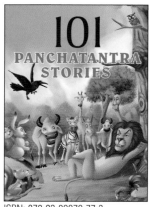

ISBN: 978-93-80070-77-3

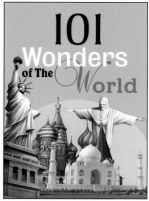

ISBN: 978-93-80070-78-0

ISBN: 978-93-81607-35-0

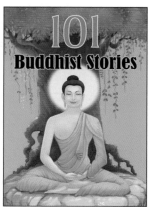

ISBN: 978-93-80069-58-6

ISBN: 978-93-80069-85-2